writing on back page *KM* 10-22-96

WITHDRAWN

S0-ABY-345

And My Mean Old Mother Will Be Sorry, Blackboard Bear

STORY AND PICTURES BY

Martha Alexander

DIAL BOOKS FOR YOUNG READERS
NEW YORK

NAPERVILLE PUBLIC LIBRARIES
Naperville, IL

a pied piper book

With special thanks to David and his teddy and to Shelly—
the three who inspired this story

Copyright © 1972 by Martha Alexander
All rights reserved. Library of Congress Catalog Card Number: 72-707
First Pied Piper Printing 1977
Printed in Hong Kong by Wing King Tong Company Ltd.
COBE
6 8 10 9 7 5
A Pied Piper Book is a registered trademark of
Dial Books for Young Readers
® TM 1,163,686 and ® TM 1,054,312
AND MY MEAN OLD MOTHER WILL BE SORRY, BLACKBOARD BEAR
is published in a hardcover edition by
Dial Books for Young Readers
2 Park Avenue, New York, New York 10016
ISBN 0-8037-0126-8

For Kimie

Boy, is she mad!

Honey? Yes, I think we have some.

No more? Me too, I'm full.

EEEEEEEEK!
Sticky honey all over
my kitchen! One little
boy named Anthony
better be in bed—
that's all I can say!

Mean old mother. Always yelling!
Can't ever have any fun in *this* house.

What? Run away? You and me?

We could live in a cave? That's great!

Let's go! No, I don't want to take my toothbrush. I'll *never* brush my teeth again. And my mean old mother will be sorry.

These blueberries are really good, but I'm still hungry.
Oh, yes, I love honey.

My mom *never* lets me eat this much, though.
She says I'd get sick.

Oh, no. I'm not sick. I think my stomach just feels that way from walking so far.

That's better. Do you think we could
find a hamburger somewhere?

No hamburger . . . just fish?
Oh, yes, I like trout.

But I don't think I can eat it
while it's wiggling.

Oh! You don't mind the wiggling?
Well, maybe I *could* get used to it.

Maybe I'll get used to the dark too,
but I wish I had brought my flashlight.

You're sure it's only an owl?
Oh, no, I'm not afraid.

Oh, you're getting sleepy?
Well, yes, a little.

This is a great cave! But what
is that fluttering noise? Oh,
I didn't know bats live in caves
too. Couldn't we have a cave of
our own? Not tonight? Oh.

I wish I had my pillow. I'm
a little cold too. You'll keep
me warm? Oh, that's better.
In the morning I better go
get my pillow and blanket.
Maybe my bed too.

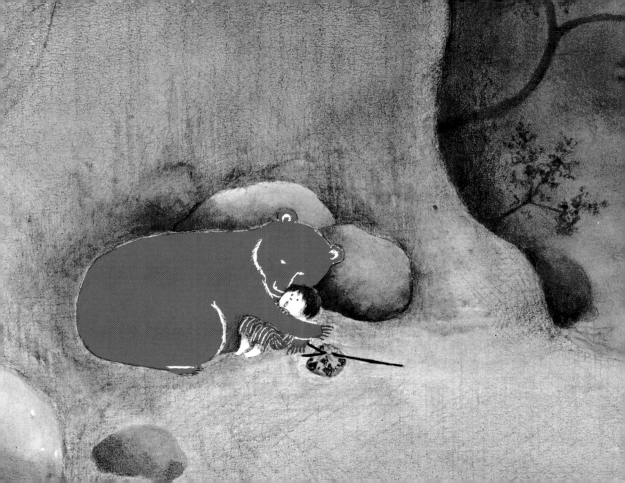

Miss me? You really think
she would? Well...no, I don't
want her to be lonesome. She's
mostly a good mom. You mean
go back? Well, all right, we'll
talk about it in the morning.
Good night.

It's getting light and I'm really hungry.
Berries for breakfast too? No orange juice
or cereal or milk? Oh.

You *really* think I should?
But I could visit you often, couldn't I?
Oh, good.

Well, good-bye. Thank you for riding me back.
Oh, yes, I can get in all right.
I'll be seeing you.

Why hello, Teddy! You really did? You missed
me a lot? You're such a good Teddy.

I love you too, Teddy.

Syria ✓

Wely ✓

Jd ✓
JP ✓

Think   walk
house   dark
sticky honey   wiggling
what   and
mean   could
sorry   should
toothbrush   sleepy
sick
hungry